The Reception of the 'Origin of Species'

Thomas Henry Huxley

Contents

THE RECEPTION OF THE 'ORIGIN OF SPECIES'

BY

Thomas Henry Huxley

ON THE RECEPTION OF THE 'ORIGIN OF SPECIES'

by

PROFESSOR THOMAS HENRY HUXLEY

FROM THE LIFE AND LETTERS OF CHARLES DARWIN

EDITED BY FRANCIS DARWIN

ON THE RECEPTION OF THE 'ORIGIN OF SPECIES.'

To the present generation, that is to say, the people a few years on
the hither and thither side of thirty, the name of Charles Darwin
stands alongside of those of Isaac Newton and Michael Faraday; and,
like them, calls up the grand ideal of a searcher after truth and
interpreter of Nature. They think of him who bore it as a rare
combination of genius, industry, and unswerving veracity, who earned
his place among the most famous men of the age by sheer native power,
in the teeth of a gale of popular prejudice, and uncheered by a sign of
favour or appreciation from the official fountains of honour; as one
who in spite of an acute sensitiveness to praise and blame, and
notwithstanding provocations which might have excused any outbreak,
kept himself clear of all envy, hatred, and malice, nor dealt otherwise
than fairly and justly with the unfairness and injustice which was
showered upon him; while, to the end of his days, he was ready to

listen with patience and respect to the most insignificant of reasonable objectors.

And with respect to that theory of the origin of the forms of life peopling our globe, with which Darwin's name is bound up as closely as that of Newton with the theory of gravitation, nothing seems to be further from the mind of the present generation than any attempt to smother it with ridicule or to crush it by vehemence of denunciation. "The struggle for existence," and "Natural selection," have become household words and every-day conceptions. The reality and the importance of the natural processes on which Darwin founds his deductions are no more doubted than those of growth and multiplication; and, whether the full potency attributed to them is admitted or not, no one doubts their vast and far-reaching significance. Wherever the biological sciences are studied, the 'Origin of Species' lights the paths of the investigator; wherever they are taught it permeates the course of instruction. Nor has the influence of Darwinian ideas been less profound, beyond the realms of Biology. The oldest of all philosophies, that of Evolution, was bound hand and foot and cast into utter darkness during the millennium of theological scholasticism. But Darwin poured new life-blood into the ancient frame; the bonds burst, and the revivified thought of ancient Greece has proved itself to be a more adequate expression of the universal order of things than any of the schemes which have been accepted by the credulity and welcomed by the superstition of seventy later generations of men.

To any one who studies the signs of the times, the emergence of the philosophy of Evolution, in the attitude of claimant to the throne of the world of thought, from the limbo of hated and, as many hoped, forgotten things, is the most portentous event of the nineteenth century. But the most effective weapons of the modern champions of Evolution were fabricated by Darwin; and the 'Origin of Species' has enlisted a formidable body of combatants, trained in the severe school of Physical Science, whose ears might have long remained deaf to the speculations of a priori philosophers.

I do not think any candid or instructed person will deny the truth of that which has just been asserted. He may hate the very name of Evolution, and may deny its pretensions as vehemently as a Jacobite denied those of George the Second. But there it is--not only as solidly seated as the Hanoverian dynasty, but happily independent of Parliamentary sanction--and the dullest antagonists have come to see that they have to deal with an adversary whose bones are to be broken by no amount of bad words.

Even the theologians have almost ceased to pit the plain meaning of Genesis against the no less plain meaning of Nature. Their more candid, or more cautious, representatives have given up dealing with Evolution as if it were a damnable heresy, and have taken refuge in one of two courses. Either they deny that Genesis was meant to teach scientific truth, and thus save the veracity of the record at the expense of its authority; or they expend their energies in devising the cruel ingenuities of the reconciler, and torture texts in the vain hope of making them confess the creed of Science. But when the peine forte et dure is over, the antique sincerity of the venerable sufferer always reasserts itself. Genesis is honest to the core, and professes to be no more than it is, a repository of venerable traditions of unknown origin, claiming no scientific authority and possessing none.

As my pen finishes these passages, I can but be amused to think what a terrible hubbub would have been made (in truth was made) about any similar expressions of opinion a quarter of a century ago. In fact, the contrast between the present condition of public opinion upon the Darwinian question; between the estimation in which Darwin's views are now held in the scientific world; between the acquiescence, or at least quiescence, of the theologians of the self-respecting order at the present day and the outburst of antagonism on all sides in 1858-9, when the new theory respecting the origin of species first became known to the older generation to which I belong, is so startling that, except for documentary evidence, I should be sometimes inclined to think my memories dreams. I have a great respect for the younger generation myself (they can write our lives, and ravel out all our follies, if they choose to take the trouble, by and by), and I should be glad to be assured that the feeling is reciprocal; but I am afraid that the story of our dealings with Darwin may prove a great hindrance to that veneration for our wisdom which I should like them to display. We have not even the excuse that, thirty years ago, Mr. Darwin was an obscure novice, who had no claims on our attention. On the contrary, his remarkable zoological and geological investigations had long given him an assured position among the most eminent and original investigators of the day; while his charming 'Voyage of a Naturalist' had justly earned him a wide-spread reputation among the general public. I doubt if there was any man then living who had a better right to expect that anything he might choose to say on such a question as the Origin of Species would be listened to with profound attention, and discussed with respect; and there was certainly no man whose personal character should have afforded a better safeguard against attacks, instinct with malignity and spiced with shameless impertinences.

Yet such was the portion of one of the kindest and truest men that it was ever my good fortune to know; and years had to pass away before misrepresentation, ridicule, and denunciation, ceased to be the most notable constituents of the majority of the multitudinous criticisms of his work which poured from the press. I am loth to rake any of these ancient scandals from their well-deserved oblivion; but I must make good a statement which may seem overcharged to the present generation, and there is no piece justificative more apt for the purpose, or more worthy of such dishonour, than the article in the 'Quarterly Review' for July, 1860. (I was not aware when I wrote these passages that the authorship of the article had been publicly acknowledged. Confession unaccompanied by penitence, however, affords no ground for mitigation of judgment; and the kindliness with which Mr. Darwin speaks of his assailant, Bishop Wilberforce (vol. ii.), is so striking an exemplification of his singular gentleness and modesty, that it rather increases one's indignation against the presumption of his critic.) Since Lord Brougham assailed Dr. Young, the world has seen no such specimen of the insolence of a shallow pretender to a Master in Science as this remarkable production, in which one of the most exact of observers, most cautious of reasoners, and most candid of expositors, of this or any other age, is held up to scorn as a "flighty" person, who endeavours "to prop up his utterly rotten fabric of guess and speculation," and whose "mode of dealing with nature" is reprobated as "utterly dishonourable to Natural Science." And all this high and mighty talk, which would have been indecent in one of Mr. Darwin's equals, proceeds from a writer whose want of intelligence, or of conscience, or of both, is so great, that, by way of an objection to Mr. Darwin's views, he can ask, "Is it credible that all favourable varieties of turnips are tending to become men;" who is so ignorant of paleontology, that he can talk of the "flowers and fruits" of the plants of the carboniferous epoch; of comparative anatomy, that he can gravely affirm the poison apparatus of the venomous snakes to be "entirely separate from the ordinary laws of animal life, and peculiar to themselves;" of the rudiments of physiology, that he can ask, "what advantage of life could alter the shape of the corpuscles into which the blood can be evaporated?" Nor does the reviewer fail to flavour this outpouring of preposterous incapacity with a little stimulation of the odium theologicum. Some inkling of the history of the conflicts between Astronomy, Geology, and Theology, leads him to keep a retreat open by the proviso that he cannot "consent to test the truth of Natural Science by the word of Revelation;" but, for all that, he devotes pages to the exposition of his conviction that Mr. Darwin's theory "contradicts the revealed relation of the creation to its

Creator," and is "inconsistent with the fulness of his glory."

If I confine my retrospect of the reception of the 'Origin of Species' to a twelvemonth, or thereabouts, from the time of its publication, I do not recollect anything quite so foolish and unmannerly as the 'Quarterly Review' article, unless, perhaps, the address of a Reverend Professor to the Dublin Geological Society might enter into competition with it. But a large proportion of Mr. Darwin's critics had a lamentable resemblance to the 'Quarterly' reviewer, in so far as they lacked either the will, or the wit, to make themselves masters of his doctrine; hardly any possessed the knowledge required to follow him through the immense range of biological and geological science which the 'Origin' covered; while, too commonly, they had prejudiced the case on theological grounds, and, as seems to be inevitable when this happens, eked out lack of reason by superfluity of railing.

But it will be more pleasant and more profitable to consider those criticisms, which were acknowledged by writers of scientific authority, or which bore internal evidence of the greater or less competency and, often, of the good faith, of their authors. Restricting my survey to a twelvemonth, or thereabouts, after the publication of the 'Origin,' I find among such critics Louis Agassiz ("The arguments presented by Darwin in favor of a universal derivation from one primary form of all the peculiarities existing now among living beings have not made the slightest impression on my mind."

"Until the facts of Nature are shown to have been mistaken by those who have collected them, and that they have a different meaning from that now generally assigned to them, I shall therefore consider the transmutation theory as a scientific mistake, untrue in its facts, unscientific in its method, and mischievous in its tendency."--Silliman's 'Journal,' July, 1860, pages 143, 154. Extract from the 3rd volume of 'Contributions to the Natural History of the

United States.'); Murray, an excellent entomologist; Harvey, a botanist of considerable repute; and the author of an article in the 'Edinburgh Review,' all strongly adverse to Darwin. Pictet, the distinguished and widely learned paleontogist of Geneva, treats Mr. Darwin with a respect which forms a grateful contrast to the tone of some of the preceding writers, but consents to go with him only a very little way. ("I see no serious objections to the formation of varieties by natural selection in the existing world, and that, so far as earlier epochs are concerned, this law may be assumed to explain the origin of closely allied species, supposing for this purpose a very long period of time."

"With regard to simple varieties and closely allied species, I believe that Mr. Darwin's theory may explain many things, and throw a great light upon numerous questions."--'Sur l'Origine de l'Espece. Par Charles Darwin.' 'Archives des Sc. de la Bibliotheque Universelle de Geneve,' pages 242, 243, Mars 1860.) On the other hand, Lyell, up to that time a pillar of the anti-transmutationists (who regarded him, ever afterwards, as Pallas Athene may have looked at Dian, after the Endymion affair), declared himself a Darwinian, though not without putting in a serious caveat. Nevertheless, he was a tower of strength, and his courageous stand for truth as against consistency, did him infinite honour. As evolutionists, sans phrase, I do not call to mind among the biologists more than Asa Gray, who fought the battle splendidly in the United States; Hooker, who was no less vigorous here; the present Sir John Lubbock and myself. Wallace was far away in the Malay Archipelago; but, apart from his direct share in the promulgation of the theory of natural selection, no enumeration of the influences at work, at the time I am speaking of, would be complete without the mention of his powerful essay 'On the Law which has regulated the Introduction of New Species,' which was published in 1855. On reading it afresh, I have been astonished to recollect how small was the impression it made.

In France, the influence of Elie de Beaumont and of Flourens--the former of whom is said to have "damned himself to everlasting fame" by inventing the nickname of "la science moussante" for Evolutionism (One is reminded of the effect of another small academic epigram. The so-called vertebral theory of the skull is said to have been nipped in the bud in France by the whisper of an academician to his neighbour, that, in that case, one's head was a "vertebre pensante."),--to say nothing of the ill-will of other powerful members of the Institut, produced for a long time the effect of a conspiracy of silence; and many years passed before the Academy redeemed itself from the reproach that the name of Darwin was not to be found on the list of its members. However, an accomplished writer, out of the range of academical influences, M. Laugel, gave an excellent and appreciative notice of the 'Origin' in the 'Revue des Deux Mondes.' Germany took time to consider; Bronn produced a slightly Bowdlerized translation of the 'Origin'; and 'Kladderadatsch' cut his jokes upon the ape origin of man; but I do not call to mind that any scientific notability declared himself publicly in 1860. (However, the man who stands next to Darwin in his influence on modern biologists, K.E. von Baer, wrote to me, in August 1860, expressing his general assent to evolutionist views. His phrase, "J'ai enonce les memes idees...que M. Darwin" (volume ii.) is shown by his subsequent writings to mean no more than this.) None of us dreamed that, in the course of a few years, the strength (and perhaps I may add the weakness) of "Darwinismus" would have its most extensive and most brilliant illustrations in the land of learning. If a foreigner may presume to speculate on the cause of this curious interval of silence, I fancy it was that one moiety of the German biologists were orthodox at any price, and the other moiety as distinctly heterodox. The latter were evolutionists, a priori, already, and they must have felt the disgust natural to deductive philosophers at being offered an inductive and experimental foundation for a conviction which they had reached by a shorter cut. It is undoubtedly trying to learn that, though your conclusions may be all right, your reasons for them are all wrong, or, at any rate, insufficient.

On the whole, then, the supporters of Mr. Darwin's views in 1860 were numerically extremely insignificant. There is not the slightest doubt that, if a general council of the Church scientific had been held at that time, we should have been condemned by an overwhelming majority. And there is as little doubt that, if such a council gathered now, the decree would be of an exactly contrary nature. It would indicate a lack of sense, as well as of modesty, to ascribe to the men of that generation less capacity or less honesty than their successors possess. What, then, are the causes which led instructed and fair-judging men of that day to arrive at a judgment so different from that which seems just and fair to those who follow them? That is really one of the most interesting of all questions connected with the history of science, and I shall try to answer it. I am afraid that in order to do so I must run the risk of appearing egotistical. However, if I tell my own story it is only because I know it better than that of other people.

I think I must have read the 'Vestiges' before I left England in 1846; but, if I did, the book made very little impression upon me, and I was not brought into serious contact with the 'Species' question until after 1850. At that time, I had long done with the Pentateuchal cosmogony, which had been impressed upon my childish understanding as Divine truth, with all the authority of parents and instructors, and from which it had cost me many a struggle to get free. But my mind was unbiassed in respect of any doctrine which presented itself, if it professed to be based on purely philosophical and scientific reasoning. It seemed to me then (as it does now) that "creation," in the ordinary sense of the word, is perfectly conceivable. I find no difficulty in imagining that, at some former period, this universe was not in existence; and that it made its appearance in six days (or instantaneously, if that is preferred), in consequence of the volition of some pre-existent Being. Then, as now, the so-called a priori arguments against Theism; and, given a Deity, against the possibility of creative acts, appeared to me to be devoid of reasonable foundation. I had not then, and I have not now, the smallest a priori objection to raise to the account of the creation of animals and plants given in 'Paradise Lost,' in which Milton so vividly embodies the natural sense of Genesis. Far be it from me to say that it is untrue because it is impossible. I confine myself to what must be regarded as a modest and reasonable request for some particle of evidence that the existing species of animals and plants did originate in that way, as a condition of my belief in a statement which appears to me to be highly improbable.

And, by way of being perfectly fair, I had exactly the same answer to give to the evolutionists of 1851-8. Within the ranks of the biologists, at that time, I met with nobody, except Dr. Grant, of University College, who had a word to say for Evolution--and his advocacy was not calculated to advance the cause. Outside these ranks, the only person known to me whose knowledge and capacity compelled respect, and who was, at the same time, a thorough-going evolutionist, was Mr. Herbert Spencer, whose acquaintance I made, I think, in 1852, and then entered into the bonds of a friendship which, I am happy to think, has known no interruption. Many and prolonged were the battles we fought on this topic. But even my friend's rare dialectic skill and copiousness of apt illustration could not drive me from my agnostic position. I took my stand upon two grounds: firstly, that up to that time, the evidence in favour of transmutation was wholly insufficient; and secondly, that no suggestion respecting the causes of the transmutation assumed, which had been made, was in any way adequate to explain the phenomena. Looking back at the state of knowledge at that time, I really do not see that any other conclusion was justifiable.

In those days I had never even heard of Treviranus' 'Biologie.' However, I had studied Lamarck attentively and I had read the

'Vestiges' with due care; but neither of them afforded me any good ground for changing my negative and critical attitude. As for the 'Vestiges,' I confess that the book simply irritated me by the prodigious ignorance and thoroughly unscientific habit of mind manifested by the writer. If it had any influence on me at all, it set me against Evolution; and the only review I ever have qualms of conscience about, on the ground of needless savagery, is one I wrote on the 'Vestiges' while under that influence.

With respect to the 'Philosophie Zoologique,' it is no reproach to Lamarck to say that the discussion of the Species question in that work, whatever might be said for it in 1809, was miserably below the level of the knowledge of half a century later. In that interval of time the elucidation of the structure of the lower animals and plants had given rise to wholly new conceptions of their relations; histology and embryology, in the modern sense, had been created; physiology had been reconstituted; the facts of distribution, geological and geographical, had been prodigiously multiplied and reduced to order. To any biologist whose studies had carried him beyond mere species-mongering in 1850, one-half of Lamarck's arguments were obsolete and the other half erroneous, or defective, in virtue of omitting to deal with the various classes of evidence which had been brought to light since his time. Moreover his one suggestion as to the cause of the gradual modification of species--effort excited by change of conditions--was, on the face of it, inapplicable to the whole vegetable world. I do not think that any impartial judge who reads the 'Philosophie Zoologique' now, and who afterwards takes up Lyell's trenchant and effectual criticism (published as far back as 1830), will be disposed to allot to Lamarck a much higher place in the establishment of biological evolution than that which Bacon assigns to himself in relation to physical science generally,--buccinator tantum. (Erasmus Darwin first promulgated Lamarck's fundamental conceptions, and, with greater logical consistency, he had applied them to plants.

But the advocates of his claims have failed to show that he, in any respect, anticipated the central idea of the 'Origin of Species.')

But, by a curious irony of fate, the same influence which led me to put as little faith in modern speculations on this subject, as in the venerable traditions recorded in the first two chapters of Genesis, was perhaps more potent than any other in keeping alive a sort of pious conviction that Evolution, after all, would turn out true. I have recently read afresh the first edition of the 'Principles of Geology'; and when I consider that this remarkable book had been nearly thirty years in everybody's hands, and that it brings home to any reader of ordinary intelligence a great principle and a great fact--the principle, that the past must be explained by the present, unless good cause be shown to the contrary; and the fact, that, so far as our knowledge of the past history of life on our globe goes, no such cause can be shown (The same principle and the same fact guide the result from all sound historical investigation. Grote's 'History of Greece' is a product of the same intellectual movement as Lyell's 'Principles.')--I cannot but believe that Lyell, for others, as for myself, was the chief agent for smoothing the road for Darwin. For consistent uniformitarianism postulates evolution as much in the organic as in the inorganic world. The origin of a new species by other than ordinary agencies would be a vastly greater "catastrophe" than any of those which Lyell successfully eliminated from sober geological speculation.

In fact, no one was better aware of this than Lyell himself. (Lyell, with perfect right, claims this position for himself. He speaks of having "advocated a law of continuity even in the organic world, so far as possible without adopting Lamarck's theory of transmutation"...

"But while I taught that as often as certain forms of animals and plants disappeared, for reasons quite intelligible to us, others took their place by virtue of a causation which was beyond our comprehension; it remained for Darwin to accumulate proof that there is no break between the incoming and the outgoing species, that they are the work of evolution, and not of special creation...

"I had certainly prepared the way in this country, in six editions of my work before the 'Vestiges of Creation' appeared in 1842 [1844], for the reception of Darwin's gradual and insensible evolution of species."--'Life and Letters,' Letter to Haeckel, volume ii. page 436. November 23, 1868.) If one reads any of the earlier editions of the 'Principles' carefully (especially by the light of the interesting series of letters recently published by Sir Charles Lyell's biographer), it is easy to see that, with all his energetic opposition to Lamarck, on the one hand, and to the ideal quasi-progressionism of Agassiz, on the other, Lyell, in his own mind, was strongly disposed to account for the origination of all past and present species of living things by natural causes. But he would have liked, at the same time, to keep the name of creation for a natural process which he imagined to be incomprehensible.

In a letter addressed to Mantell (dated March 2, 1827), Lyell speaks of having just read Lamarck; he expresses his delight at Lamarck's theories, and his personal freedom from any objection based on theological grounds. And though he is evidently alarmed at the pithecoid origin of man involved in Lamarck's doctrine, he observes:--

"But, after all, what changes species may really undergo! How impossible will it be to distinguish and lay down a line, beyond which some of the so-called extinct species have never passed into recent ones."

Again, the following remarkable passage occurs in the postscript of a letter addressed to Sir John Herschel in 1836:--

"In regard to the origination of new species, I am very glad to find that you think it probable that it may be carried on through the intervention of intermediate causes. I left this rather to be inferred, not thinking it worth while to offend a certain class of persons by embodying in words what would only be a speculation." (In the same sense, see the letter to Whewell, March 7, 1837, volume ii., page 5:--

"In regard to this last subject [the changes from one set of animal and vegetable species to another]...you remember what Herschel said in his letter to me. If I had stated as plainly as he has done the possibility of the introduction or origination of fresh species being a natural, in contradistinction to a miraculous process, I should have raised a host of prejudices against me, which are unfortunately opposed at every step to any philosopher who attempts to address the public on these mysterious subjects." See also letter to Sedgwick, January 12, 1838 ii. page 35.) He goes on to refer to the criticisms which have been directed against him on the ground that, by leaving species to be originated by miracle, he is inconsistent with his own doctrine of uniformitarianism; and he leaves it to be understood that he had not replied, on the ground of his general objection to controversy.

Lyell's contemporaries were not without some inkling of his esoteric doctrine. Whewell's 'History of the Inductive Sciences,' whatever its philosophical value, is always worth reading and always interesting, if under no other aspect than that of an evidence of the speculative limits within which a highly-placed divine might, at that time, safely range at will. In the course of his discussion of uniformitarianism, the encyclopaedic Master of Trinity observes:--

"Mr. Lyell, indeed, has spoken of an hypothesis that 'the successive creation of species may constitute a regular part of the economy of nature,' but he has nowhere, I think, so described this process as to make it appear in what department of science we are to place the hypothesis. Are these new species created by the production, at long intervals, of an offspring different in species from the parents? Or are the species so created produced without parents? Are they gradually evolved from some embryo substance? Or do they suddenly start from the ground, as in the creation of the poet?...

"Some selection of one of these forms of the hypothesis, rather than the others, with evidence for the selection, is requisite to entitle us to place it among the known causes of change, which in this chapter we are considering. The bare conviction that a creation of species has taken place, whether once or many times, so long as it is unconnected with our organical sciences, is a tenet of Natural Theology rather than of Physical Philosophy." (Whewell's 'History,' volume iii. page 639-640 (Edition 2, 1847.))

The earlier part of this criticism appears perfectly just and appropriate; but, from the concluding paragraph, Whewell evidently imagines that by "creation" Lyell means a preternatural intervention of the Deity; whereas the letter to Herschel shows that, in his own mind, Lyell meant natural causation; and I see no reason to doubt (The following passages in Lyell's letters appear to me decisive on this point:--

To Darwin, October 3, 1859 (ii, 325), on first reading the 'Origin.'

"I have long seen most clearly that if any concession is made, all that you claim in your concluding pages will follow.

"It is this which has made me so long hesitate, always feeling that the case of Man and his Races, and of other animals, and that of plants, is one and the same, and that if a vera causa be admitted for one instant, [instead] of a purely unknown and imaginary one, such as the word 'creation,' all the consequences must follow."

To Darwin, March 15, 1863 (volume ii. page 365).

"I remember that it was the conclusion he [Lamarck] came to about man that fortified me thirty years ago against the great impression which his arguments at first made on my mind, all the greater because Constant Prevost, a pupil of Cuvier's forty years ago, told me his conviction 'that Cuvier thought species not real, but that science could not advance without assuming that they were so.'"

To Hooker, March 9, 1863 (volume ii. page 361), in reference to Darwin's feeling about the 'Antiquity of Man.'

"He [Darwin] seems much disappointed that I do not go farther with him, or do not speak out more. I can only say that I have spoken out to the full extent of my present convictions, and even beyond my state of FEELING as to man's unbroken descent from the brutes, and I find I am half converting not a few who were in arms against Darwin, and are even now against Huxley." He speaks of having had to abandon "old and long cherished ideas, which constituted the charm to me of the theoretical part of the science in my earlier day, when I believed with Pascal in the theory, as Hallam terms it, of 'the arch-angel ruined.'"

See the same sentiment in the letter to Darwin, March 11, 1863, page 363:--

"I think the old 'creation' is almost as much required as ever, but of course it takes a new form if Lamarck's views improved by yours are adopted.") that, if Sir Charles could have avoided the inevitable corollary of the pithecoid origin of man--for which, to the end of his life, he entertained a profound antipathy--he would have advocated the efficiency of causes now in operation to bring about the condition of the organic world, as stoutly as he championed that doctrine in reference to inorganic nature.

The fact is, that a discerning eye might have seen that some form or other of the doctrine of transmutation was inevitable, from the time when the truth enunciated by William Smith that successive strata are characterised by different kinds of fossil remains, became a firmly established law of nature. No one has set forth the speculative consequences of this generalisation better than the historian of the 'Inductive Sciences':--

"But the study of geology opens to us the spectacle of many groups of species which have, in the course of the earth's history, succeeded each other at vast intervals of time; one set of animals and plants disappearing, as it would seem, from the face of our planet, and others, which did not before exist, becoming the only occupants of the globe. And the dilemma then presents itself to us anew:--either we must accept the doctrine of the transmutation of species, and must suppose that the organized species of one geological epoch were transmuted into those of another by some long-continued agency of natural causes; or else, we must believe in many successive acts of creation and extinction of species, out of the common course of nature; acts which, therefore, we may properly call miraculous." (Whewell's 'History of the Inductive Sciences.' Edition ii., 1847, volume iii. pages 624-625. See for the author's verdict, pages 638-39.)

Dr. Whewell decides in favour of the latter conclusion. And if any one had plied him with the four questions which he puts to Lyell in the passage already cited, all that can be said now is that he would certainly have rejected the first. But would he really have had the courage to say that a Rhinoceros tichorhinus, for instance, "was produced without parents;" or was "evolved from some embryo substance;"

or that it suddenly started from the ground like Milton's lion "pawing to get free his hinder parts." I permit myself to doubt whether even the Master of Trinity's well-tried courage--physical, intellectual, and moral--would have been equal to this feat. No doubt the sudden concurrence of half-a-ton of inorganic molecules into a live rhinoceros is conceivable, and therefore may be possible. But does such an event lie sufficiently within the bounds of probability to justify the belief in its occurrence on the strength of any attainable, or, indeed, imaginable, evidence?

In view of the assertion (often repeated in the early days of the opposition to Darwin) that he had added nothing to Lamarck, it is very interesting to observe that the possibility of a fifth alternative, in addition to the four he has stated, has not dawned upon Dr. Whewell's mind. The suggestion that new species may result from the selective action of external conditions upon the variations from their specific type which individuals present--and which we call "spontaneous," because we are ignorant of their causation--is as wholly unknown to the historian of scientific ideas as it was to biological specialists before 1858. But that suggestion is the central idea of the 'Origin of Species,' and contains the quintessence of Darwinism.

Thus, looking back into the past, it seems to me that my own position of critical expectancy was just and reasonable, and must have been taken up, on the same grounds, by many other persons. If Agassiz told me that the forms of life which had successively tenanted the globe were the incarnations of successive thoughts of the Deity; and that he had wiped out one set of these embodiments by an appalling geological catastrophe as soon as His ideas took a more advanced shape, I found myself not only unable to admit the accuracy of the deductions from the facts of paleontology, upon which this astounding hypothesis was founded, but I had to confess my want of any means of testing the correctness of his explanation of them. And besides that, I could by no means see what the explanation explained. Neither did it help me to be told by an eminent anatomist that species had succeeded one another in time, in virtue of "a continuously operative creational law." That seemed to me to be no more than saying that species had succeeded one another, in the form of a vote-catching resolution, with "law" to please the man of science, and "creational" to draw the orthodox. So I took refuge in that "thatige Skepsis" which Goethe has so well defined; and, reversing the apostolic precept to be all things to all men, I usually defended the tenability of the received doctrines, when I had to do with the transmutationists; and stood up for the possibility of transmutation among the orthodox--thereby, no doubt, increasing an already current, but quite undeserved, reputation for needless combativeness.

I remember, in the course of my first interview with Mr. Darwin, expressing my belief in the sharpness of the lines of demarcation between natural groups and in the absence of transitional forms, with all the confidence of youth and imperfect knowledge. I was not aware, at that time, that he had then been many years brooding over the species-question; and the humorous smile which accompanied his gentle answer, that such was not altogether his view, long haunted and puzzled me. But it would seem that four or five years' hard work had enabled me to understand what it meant; for Lyell ('Life and Letters,' volume ii. page 212.), writing to Sir Charles Bunbury (under date of April 30, 1856), says:--

"When Huxley, Hooker, and Wollaston were at Darwin's last week they (all four of them) ran a tilt against species--further, I believe, than they are prepared to go."

I recollect nothing of this beyond the fact of meeting Mr. Wollaston; and except for Sir Charles' distinct assurance as to "all four," I should have thought my "outrecuidance" was probably a counterblast to

Wollaston's conservatism. With regard to Hooker, he was already, like
Voltaire's Habbakuk, "capable du tout" in the way of advocating
Evolution.

As I have already said, I imagine that most of those of my
contemporaries who thought seriously about the matter, were very much
in my own state of mind--inclined to say to both Mosaists and
Evolutionists, "a plague on both your houses!" and disposed to turn
aside from an interminable and apparently fruitless discussion, to
labour in the fertile fields of ascertainable fact. And I may,
therefore, further suppose that the publication of the Darwin and
Wallace papers in 1858, and still more that of the 'Origin' in 1859,
had the effect upon them of the flash of light, which to a man who has
lost himself in a dark night, suddenly reveals a road which, whether it
takes him straight home or not, certainly goes his way. That which we
were looking for, and could not find, was a hypothesis respecting the
origin of known organic forms, which assumed the operation of no causes
but such as could be proved to be actually at work. We wanted, not to
pin our faith to that or any other speculation, but to get hold of
clear and definite conceptions which could be brought face to face with
facts and have their validity tested. The 'Origin' provided us with
the working hypothesis we sought. Moreover, it did the immense service
of freeing us for ever from the dilemma--refuse to accept the creation
hypothesis, and what have you to propose that can be accepted by any
cautious reasoner? In 1857, I had no answer ready, and I do not think
that any one else had. A year later, we reproached ourselves with
dullness for being perplexed by such an inquiry. My reflection, when I
first made myself master of the central idea of the 'Origin,' was, "How
extremely stupid not to have thought of that!" I suppose that
Columbus' companions said much the same when he made the egg stand on
end. The facts of variability, of the struggle for existence, of
adaptation to conditions, were notorious enough; but none of us had
suspected that the road to the heart of the species problem lay through

them, until Darwin and Wallace dispelled the darkness, and the beacon-fire of the 'Origin' guided the benighted.

Whether the particular shape which the doctrine of evolution, as applied to the organic world, took in Darwin's hands, would prove to be final or not, was, to me, a matter of indifference. In my earliest criticisms of the 'Origin' I ventured to point out that its logical foundation was insecure so long as experiments in selective breeding had not produced varieties which were more or less infertile; and that insecurity remains up to the present time. But, with any and every critical doubt which my sceptical ingenuity could suggest, the Darwinian hypothesis remained incomparably more probable than the creation hypothesis. And if we had none of us been able to discern the paramount significance of some of the most patent and notorious of natural facts, until they were, so to speak, thrust under our noses, what force remained in the dilemma--creation or nothing? It was obvious that, hereafter, the probability would be immensely greater, that the links of natural causation were hidden from our purblind eyes, than that natural causation should be incompetent to produce all the phenomena of nature. The only rational course for those who had no other object than the attainment of truth, was to accept "Darwinism" as a working hypothesis, and see what could be made of it. Either it would prove its capacity to elucidate the facts of organic life, or it would break down under the strain. This was surely the dictate of common sense; and, for once, common sense carried the day. The result has been that complete volte-face of the whole scientific world, which must seem so surprising to the present generation. I do not mean to say that all the leaders of biological science have avowed themselves Darwinians; but I do not think that there is a single zoologist, or botanist, or palaeontologist, among the multitude of active workers of this generation, who is other than an evolutionist, profoundly influenced by Darwin's views. Whatever may be the ultimate fate of the particular theory put forth by Darwin, I venture to affirm that, so far as my knowledge goes, all the ingenuity and all the learning of hostile critics have not enabled them to adduce a solitary fact, of which it can be said, this is irreconcilable with the Darwinian theory. In the prodigious variety and complexity of organic nature, there are multitudes of phenomena which are not deducible from any generalisations we have yet reached. But the same may be said of every other class of natural objects. I believe that astronomers cannot yet get the moon's motions into perfect accordance with the theory of gravitation.

It would be inappropriate, even if it were possible, to discuss the difficulties and unresolved problems which have hitherto met the evolutionist, and which will probably continue to puzzle him for generations to come, in the course of this brief history of the reception of Mr. Darwin's great work. But there are two or three objections of a more general character, based, or supposed to be based, upon philosophical and theological foundations, which were loudly expressed in the early days of the Darwinian controversy, and which, though they have been answered over and over again, crop up now and then to the present day.

The most singular of these, perhaps immortal, fallacies, which live on, Tithonus-like, when sense and force have long deserted them, is that which charges Mr. Darwin with having attempted to reinstate the old pagan goddess, Chance. It is said that he supposes variations to come about "by chance," and that the fittest survive the "chances" of the struggle for existence, and thus "chance" is substituted for providential design.

It is not a little wonderful that such an accusation as this should be brought against a writer who has, over and over again, warned his readers that when he uses the word "spontaneous," he merely means that he is ignorant of the cause of that which is so termed; and whose whole theory crumbles to pieces if the uniformity and regularity of natural causation for illimitable past ages is denied. But probably the best answer to those who talk of Darwinism meaning the reign of "chance," is to ask them what they themselves understand by "chance"? Do they believe that anything in this universe happens without reason or without a cause? Do they really conceive that any event has no cause, and could not have been predicted by any one who had a sufficient insight into the order of Nature? If they do, it is they who are the inheritors of antique superstition and ignorance, and whose minds have never been illumined by a ray of scientific thought. The one act of faith in the convert to science, is the confession of the universality of order and of the absolute validity in all times and under all circumstances, of the law of causation. This confession is an act of faith, because, by the nature of the case, the truth of such propositions is not susceptible of proof. But such faith is not blind, but reasonable; because it is invariably confirmed by experience, and constitutes the sole trustworthy foundation for all action.

If one of these people, in whom the chance-worship of our remoter ancestors thus strangely survives, should be within reach of the sea when a heavy gale is blowing, let him betake himself to the shore and watch the scene. Let him note the infinite variety of form and size of the tossing waves out at sea; or of the curves of their foam-crested breakers, as they dash against the rocks; let him listen to the roar and scream of the shingle as it is cast up and torn down the beach; or look at the flakes of foam as they drive hither and thither before the wind; or note the play of colours, which answers a gleam of sunshine as it falls upon the myriad bubbles. Surely here, if anywhere, he will say that chance is supreme, and bend the knee as one who has entered the very penetralia of his divinity. But the man of science knows that here, as everywhere, perfect order is manifested; that there is not a curve of the waves, not a note in the howling chorus, not a rainbow-glint on a bubble, which is other than a necessary consequence of the ascertained laws of nature; and that with a sufficient knowledge of the conditions, competent physico-mathematical skill could account for, and indeed predict, every one of these "chance" events.

A second very common objection to Mr. Darwin's views was (and is), that they abolish Teleology, and eviscerate the argument from design. It is nearly twenty years since I ventured to offer some remarks on this subject, and as my arguments have as yet received no refutation, I hope I may be excused for reproducing them. I observed, "that the doctrine of Evolution is the most formidable opponent of all the commoner and coarser forms of Teleology. But perhaps the most remarkable service to the Philosophy of Biology rendered by Mr. Darwin is the reconciliation of Teleology and Morphology, and the explanation of the facts of both, which his views offer. The teleology which supposes that the eye, such as we see it in man, or one of the higher vertebrata, was made with the precise structure it exhibits, for the purpose of enabling the animal which possesses it to see, has undoubtedly received its death-blow. Nevertheless, it is necessary to remember that there is a wider teleology which is not touched by the doctrine of Evolution, but is actually based upon the fundamental proposition of Evolution. This proposition is that the whole world, living and not living, is the result of the mutual interaction, according to definite laws, of the forces (I should now like to substitute the word powers for "forces.") possessed by the molecules of which the primitive nebulosity of the universe was composed. If this be true, it is no less certain that the existing world lay potentially in the cosmic vapour, and that a sufficient intelligence could, from a knowledge of the properties of the molecules of that vapour, have predicted, say the state of the fauna of Britain in 1869, with as much certainty as one can say what will happen to the vapour of the breath on a cold winter's day...

...The teleological and the mechanical views of nature are not, necessarily, mutually exclusive. On the contrary, the more purely a mechanist the speculator is, the more firmly does he assume a primordial molecular arrangement of which all the phenomena of the universe are the consequences, and the more completely is he thereby at the mercy of the teleologist, who can always defy him to disprove that this primordial molecular arrangement was not intended to evolve the phenomena of the universe." (The "Genealogy of Animals" ('The Academy,' 1869), reprinted in 'Critiques and Addresses.')

The acute champion of Teleology, Paley, saw no difficulty in admitting that the "production of things" may be the result of trains of mechanical dispositions fixed beforehand by intelligent appointment and kept in action by a power at the centre ('Natural Theology,' chapter xxiii.), that is to say, he proleptically accepted the modern doctrine of Evolution; and his successors might do well to follow their leader, or at any rate to attend to his weighty reasonings, before rushing into an antagonism which has no reasonable foundation.

Having got rid of the belief in chance and the disbelief in design, as in no sense appurtenances of Evolution, the third libel upon that doctrine, that it is anti-theistic, might perhaps be left to shift for itself. But the persistence with which many people refuse to draw the plainest consequences from the propositions they profess to accept, renders it advisable to remark that the doctrine of Evolution is neither Anti-theistic nor Theistic. It simply has no more to do with Theism than the first book of Euclid has. It is quite certain that a normal fresh-laid egg contains neither cock nor hen; and it is also as certain as any proposition in physics or morals, that if such an egg is kept under proper conditions for three weeks, a cock or hen chicken will be found in it. It is also quite certain that if the shell were transparent we should be able to watch the formation of the young fowl, day by day, by a process of evolution, from a microscopic cellular germ to its full size and complication of structure. Therefore Evolution, in the strictest sense, is actually going on in this and analogous millions and millions of instances, wherever living creatures exist. Therefore, to borrow an argument from Butler, as that which now happens must be consistent with the attributes of the Deity, if such a Being exists, Evolution must be consistent with those attributes. And, if so, the evolution of the universe, which is neither more nor less explicable than that of a chicken, must also be consistent with them. The doctrine of Evolution, therefore, does not even come into contact with Theism, considered as a philosophical doctrine. That with which it does collide, and with which it is absolutely inconsistent, is the conception of creation, which theological speculators have based upon the history narrated in the opening of the book of Genesis.

There is a great deal of talk and not a little lamentation about the so-called religious difficulties which physical science has created. In theological science, as a matter of fact, it has created none. Not a solitary problem presents itself to the philosophical Theist, at the present day, which has not existed from the time that philosophers began to think out the logical grounds and the logical consequences of Theism. All the real or imaginary perplexities which flow from the conception of the universe as a determinate mechanism, are equally involved in the assumption of an Eternal, Omnipotent and Omniscient Deity. The theological equivalent of the scientific conception of order is Providence; and the doctrine of determinism follows as surely from the attributes of foreknowledge assumed by the theologian, as from the universality of natural causation assumed by the man of science. The angels in 'Paradise Lost' would have found the task of enlightening Adam upon the mysteries of "Fate, Foreknowledge, and Free-will," not a whit more difficult, if their pupil had been educated in a "Real-schule" and trained in every laboratory of a modern university. In respect of the great problems of Philosophy, the post-Darwinian generation is, in one sense, exactly where the prae-Darwinian generations were. They remain insoluble. But the present generation has the advantage of being better provided with the means of freeing itself from the tyranny of certain sham solutions.

The known is finite, the unknown infinite; intellectually we stand on an islet in the midst of an illimitable ocean of inexplicability. Our business in every generation is to reclaim a little more land, to add something to the extent and the solidity of our possessions. And even a cursory glance at the history of the biological sciences during the last quarter of a century is sufficient to justify the assertion, that the most potent instrument for the extension of the realm of natural knowledge which has come into men's hands, since the publication of Newton's 'Principia,' is Darwin's 'Origin of Species.'

It was badly received by the generation to which it was first addressed, and the outpouring of angry nonsense to which it gave rise is sad to think upon. But the present generation will probably behave just as badly if another Darwin should arise, and inflict upon them that which the generality of mankind most hate--the necessity of revising their convictions. Let them, then, be charitable to us ancients; and if they behave no better than the men of my day to some new benefactor, let them recollect that, after all, our wrath did not come to much, and vented itself chiefly in the bad language of sanctimonious scolds. Let them as speedily perform a strategic right-about-face, and follow the truth wherever it leads. The opponents of the new truth will discover, as those of Darwin are doing, that, after all, theories do not alter facts, and that the universe remains unaffected even though texts crumble. Or, it may be, that, as history repeats itself, their happy ingenuity will also discover that the new wine is exactly of the same vintage as the old, and that (rightly viewed) the old bottles prove to have been expressly made for holding it.

The Codes Of Hammurabi And Moses
W. W. Davies

QTY

The discovery of the Hammurabi Code is one of the greatest achievements of archaeology, and is of paramount interest, not only to the student of the Bible, but also to all those interested in ancient history...

Religion   **ISBN:** *1-59462-338-4*   **Pages:132**

MSRP $12.95

The Theory of Moral Sentiments
Adam Smith

QTY

This work from 1749. contains original theories of conscience amd moral judgment and it is the foundation for systemof morals.

Philosophy **ISBN:** *1-59462-777-0*   **Pages:536**

MSRP $19.95

Jessica's First Prayer
Hesba Stretton

QTY

In a screened and secluded corner of one of the many railway-bridges which span the streets of London there could be seen a few years ago, from five o'clock every morning until half past eight, a tidily set-out coffee-stall, consisting of a trestle and board, upon which stood two large tin cans, with a small fire of charcoal burning under each so as to keep the coffee boiling during the early hours of the morning when the work-people were thronging into the city on their way to their daily toil...

Pages:84

Childrens   **ISBN:** *1-59462-373-2*   *MSRP $9.95*

My Life and Work
Henry Ford

QTY

Henry Ford revolutionized the world with his implementation of mass production for the Model T automobile. Gain valuable business insight into his life and work with his own auto-biography... "We have only started on our development of our country we have not as yet, with all our talk of wonderful progress, done more than scratch the surface. The progress has been wonderful enough but..."

Pages:300

Biographies/   **ISBN:** *1-59462-198-5*   *MSRP $21.95*

The Art of Cross-Examination
Francis Wellman

QTY

I presume it is the experience of every author, after his first book is published upon an important subject, to be almost overwhelmed with a wealth of ideas and illustrations which could readily have been included in his book, and which to his own mind, at least, seem to make a second edition inevitable. Such certainly was the case with me; and when the first edition had reached its sixth impression in five months, I rejoiced to learn that it seemed to my publishers that the book had met with a sufficiently favorable reception to justify a second and considerably enlarged edition. ..

Pages:412

Reference   **ISBN: *1-59462-647-2***   *MSRP $19.95*

On the Duty of Civil Disobedience
Henry David Thoreau

QTY

Thoreau wrote his famous essay, On the Duty of Civil Disobedience, as a protest against an unjust but popular war and the immoral but popular institution of slave-owning. He did more than write—he declined to pay his taxes, and was hauled off to gaol in consequence. Who can say how much this refusal of his hastened the end of the war and of slavery ?

Law   **ISBN: *1-59462-747-9***   **Pages:48**

MSRP $7.45

Dream Psychology
Psychoanalysis for Beginners

Sigmund Freud

Dream Psychology Psychoanalysis for Beginners
Sigmund Freud

QTY

Sigmund Freud, born Sigismund Schlomo Freud (May 6, 1856 - September 23, 1939), was a Jewish-Austrian neurologist and psychiatrist who co-founded the psychoanalytic school of psychology. Freud is best known for his theories of the unconscious mind, especially involving the mechanism of repression; his redefinition of sexual desire as mobile and directed towards a wide variety of objects; and his therapeutic techniques, especially his understanding of transference in the therapeutic relationship and the presumed value of dreams as sources of insight into unconscious desires.

Pages:196

Psychology   **ISBN: *1-59462-905-6***   *MSRP $15.45*

The Miracle of Right Thought
Orison Swett Marden

QTY

Believe with all of your heart that you will do what you were made to do. When the mind has once formed the habit of holding cheerful, happy, prosperous pictures, it will not be easy to form the opposite habit. It does not matter how improbable or how far away this realization may see, or how dark the prospects may be, if we visualize them as best we can, as vividly as possible, hold tenaciously to them and vigorously struggle to attain them, they will gradually become actualized, realized in the life. But a desire, a longing without endeavor, a yearning abandoned or held indifferently will vanish without realization.

Pages:360

Self Help   **ISBN: *1-59462-644-8***   *MSRP $25.45*

QTY

The Rosicrucian Cosmo-Conception Mystic Christianity *by Max Heindel* ISBN: *1-59462-188-8* **$38.95**
The Rosicrucian Cosmo-conception is not dogmatic, neither does it appeal to any other authority than the reason of the student. It is: not controversial, but is: sent forth in the, hope that it may help to clear... New Age/Religion Pages 646

Abandonment To Divine Providence *by Jean-Pierre de Caussade* ISBN: *1-59462-228-0* **$25.95**
"The Rev. Jean Pierre de Caussade was one of the most remarkable spiritual writers of the Society of Jesus in France in the 18th Century. His death took place at Toulouse in 1751. His works have gone through many editions and have been republished... Inspirational/Religion Pages 400

Mental Chemistry *by Charles Haanel* ISBN: *1-59462-192-6* **$23.95**
Mental Chemistry allows the change of material conditions by combining and appropriately utilizing the power of the mind. Much like applied chemistry creates something new and unique out of careful combinations of chemicals the mastery of mental chemistry... New Age Pages 354

The Letters of Robert Browning and Elizabeth Barret Barrett 1845-1846 vol II ISBN: *1-59462-193-4* **$35.95**
by Robert Browning and Elizabeth Barrett Biographies Pages 596

Gleanings In Genesis (volume I) *by Arthur W. Pink* ISBN: *1-59462-130-6* **$27.45**
Appropriately has Genesis been termed "the seed plot of the Bible" for in it we have, in germ form, almost all of the great doctrines which are afterwards fully developed in the books of Scripture which follow... Religion/Inspirational Pages 420

The Master Key *by L. W. de Laurence* ISBN: *1-59462-001-6* **$30.95**
In no branch of human knowledge has there been a more lively increase of the spirit of research during the past few years than in the study of Psychology, Concentration and Mental Discipline. The requests for authentic lessons in Thought Control, Mental Discipline and... New Age/Business Pages 422

The Lesser Key Of Solomon Goetia *by L. W. de Laurence* ISBN: *1-59462-092-X* **$9.95**
This translation of the first book of the "Lernegton" which is now for the first time made accessible to students of Talismanic Magic was done, after careful collation and edition, from numerous Ancient Manuscripts in Hebrew, Latin, and French... New Age/Occult Pages 92

Rubaiyat Of Omar Khayyam *by Edward Fitzgerald* ISBN:*1-59462-332-5* **$13.95**
Edward Fitzgerald, whom the world has already learned, in spite of his own efforts to remain within the shadow of anonymity, to look upon as one of the rarest poets of the century, was born at Bredfield, in Suffolk, on the 31st of March, 1809. He was the third son of John Purcell... Music Pages 172

Ancient Law *by Henry Maine* ISBN: *1-59462-128-4* **$29.95**
The chief object of the following pages is to indicate some of the earliest ideas of mankind, as they are reflected in Ancient Law, and to point out the relation of those ideas to modern thought. Religion/History Pages 452

Far-Away Stories *by William J. Locke* ISBN: *1-59462-129-2* **$19.45**
"Good wine needs no bush, but a collection of mixed vintages does. And this book is just such a collection. Some of the stories I do not want to remain buried for ever in the museum files of dead magazine-numbers an author's not unpardonable vanity..." Fiction Pages 272

Life of David Crockett *by David Crockett* ISBN: *1-59462-250-7* **$27.45**
"Colonel David Crockett was one of the most remarkable men of the times in which he lived. Born in humble life, but gifted with a strong will, an indomitable courage, and unremitting perseverance... Biographies/New Age Pages 424

Lip-Reading *by Edward Nitchie* ISBN: *1-59462-206-X* **$25.95**
Edward B. Nitchie, founder of the New York School for the Hard of Hearing, now the Nitchie School of Lip-Reading, Inc, wrote "LIP-READING Principles and Practice". The development and perfecting of this meritorious work on lip-reading was an undertaking... How-to Pages 400

A Handbook of Suggestive Therapeutics, Applied Hypnotism, Psychic Science ISBN: *1-59462-214-0* **$24.95**
by Henry Munro Health/New Age/Health/Self-help Pages 376

A Doll's House: and Two Other Plays *by Henrik Ibsen* ISBN: *1-59462-112-8* **$19.95**
Henrik Ibsen created this classic when in revolutionary 1848 Rome. Introducing some striking concepts in playwriting for the realist genre, this play has been studied the world over. Fiction/Classics/Plays 308

The Light of Asia *by sir Edwin Arnold* ISBN: *1-59462-204-3* **$13.95**
In this poetic masterpiece, Edwin Arnold describes the life and teachings of Buddha. The man who was to become known as Buddha to the world was born as Prince Gautama of India but he rejected the worldly riches and abandoned the reigns of power when... Religion/History/Biographies Pages 170

The Complete Works of Guy de Maupassant *by Guy de Maupassant* ISBN: *1-59462-157-8* **$16.95**
"For days and days, nights and nights, I had dreamed of that first kiss which was to consecrate our engagement, and I knew not on what spot I should put my lips..." Fiction/Classics Pages 240

The Art of Cross-Examination *by Francis L. Wellman* ISBN: *1-59462-309-0* **$26.95**
Written by a renowned trial lawyer, Wellman imparts his experience and uses case studies to explain how to use psychology to extract desired information through questioning. How-to/Science/Reference Pages 408

Answered or Unanswered? *by Louisa Vaughan* ISBN: *1-59462-248-5* **$10.95**
Miracles of Faith in China Religion Pages 112

The Edinburgh Lectures on Mental Science (1909) *by Thomas* ISBN: *1-59462-008-3* **$11.95**
This book contains the substance of a course of lectures recently given by the writer in the Queen Street Hall, Edinburgh. Its purpose is to indicate the Natural Principles governing the relation between Mental Action and Material Conditions... New Age/Psychology Pages 148

Ayesha *by H. Rider Haggard* ISBN: *1-59462-301-5* **$24.95**
Verily and indeed it is the unexpected that happens! Probably if there was one person upon the earth from whom the Editor of this, and of a certain previous history, did not expect to hear again... Classics Pages 380

Ayala's Angel *by Anthony Trollope* ISBN: *1-59462-352-X* **$29.95**
The two girls were both pretty, but Lucy who was twenty-one who supposed to be simple and comparatively unattractive, whereas Ayala was credited, as her Bombwhat romantic name might show, with poetic charm and a taste for romance. Ayala when her father died was nineteen... Fiction Pages 484

The American Commonwealth *by James Bryce* ISBN: *1-59462-286-8* **$34.45**
An interpretation of American democratic political theory. It examines political mechanics and society from the perspective of Scotsman James Bryce Politics Pages 572

Stories of the Pilgrims *by Margaret P. Pumphrey* ISBN: *1-59462-116-0* **$17.95**
This book explores pilgrims religious oppression in England as well as their escape to Holland and eventual crossing to America on the Mayflower, and their early days in New England... History Pages 268

QTY

The Fasting Cure *by Sinclair Upton*   ISBN: *1-59462-222-1*   **$13.95**

In the Cosmopolitan Magazine for May, 1910, and in the Contemporary Review (London) for April, 1910, I published an article dealing with my experiences in fasting. I have written a great many magazine articles, but never one which attracted so much attention...   New Age/Self Help/Health Pages 164

Hebrew Astrology *by Sepharial*   ISBN: *1-59462-308-2*   **$13.45**

In these days of advanced thinking it is a matter of common observation that we have left many of the old landmarks behind and that we are now pressing forward to greater heights and to a wider horizon than that which represented the mind-content of our progenitors...   Astrology Pages 144

Thought Vibration or The Law of Attraction in the Thought World   ISBN: *1-59462-127-6*   **$12.95**

by William Walker Atkinson   Psychology/Religion Pages 144

Optimism *by Helen Keller*   ISBN: *1-59462-108-X*   **$15.95**

Helen Keller was blind, deaf, and mute since 19 months old, yet famously learned how to overcome these handicaps, communicate with the world, and spread her lectures promoting optimism. An inspiring read for everyone...   Biographies/Inspirational Pages 84

Sara Crewe *by Frances Burnett*   ISBN: *1-59462-360-0*   **$9.45**

In the first place, Miss Minchin lived in London. Her home was a large, dull, tall one, in a large, dull square, where all the houses were alike, and all the sparrows were alike, and where all the door-knockers made the same heavy sound...   Childrens/Classic Pages 88

The Autobiography of Benjamin Franklin *by Benjamin Franklin*   ISBN: *1-59462-135-7*   **$24.95**

The Autobiography of Benjamin Franklin has probably been more extensively read than any other American historical work, and no other book of its kind has had such ups and downs of fortune. Franklin lived for many years in England, where he was agent...   Biographies/History Pages 332

Name	
Email	
Telephone	
Address	
City, State ZIP	

☐ Credit Card   ☐ Check / Money Order

Credit Card Number	
Expiration Date	
Signature	

Please Mail to: Book Jungle
PO Box 2226
Champaign, IL 61825
or Fax to: 630-214-0564

ORDERING INFORMATION

web: *www.bookjungle.com*
email: *sales@bookjungle.com*
fax: *630-214-0564*
mail: *Book Jungle PO Box 2226 Champaign, IL 61825*
or PayPal *to sales@bookjungle.com*

Please contact us for bulk discounts

DIRECT-ORDER TERMS

20% Discount if You Order Two or More Books
Free Domestic Shipping!
Accepted: Master Card, Visa,
Discover, American Express